Savina
THE GYPSY DANCER

Ann Tompert   ILLUSTRATED BY *Dennis Nolan*

MACMILLAN PUBLISHING COMPANY   NEW YORK

COLLIER MACMILLAN CANADA   TORONTO

MAXWELL MACMILLAN INTERNATIONAL PUBLISHING GROUP

NEW YORK   OXFORD   SINGAPORE   SYDNEY

Text copyright © 1991 by Ann Tompert • Illustrations copyright © 1991 by Dennis Nolan • Calligraphy by Leah Palmer Preiss • All rights reserved. No part of this book may be reproduced or transmitted in any form or by any means, electronic or mechanical, including photocopying, recording, or by any information storage and retrieval system, without permission in writing from the Publisher. Macmillan Publishing Company, 866 Third Avenue, New York, NY 10022. Collier Macmillan Canada, Inc., 1200 Eglinton Avenue East, Suite 200, Don Mills, Ontario M3C 3N1.

Printed and bound in Hong Kong   First Edition   10   9   8   7   6   5   4   3   2   1

The text of this book is set in 13 point Palatino. The illustrations are rendered in acrylic. • Library of Congress Cataloging-in-Publication Data • Tompert, Ann. Savina, the Gypsy dancer / Ann Tompert; illustrated by Dennis Nolan. — 1st ed.   p.   cm. Summary: Savina, a gypsy girl, captivates everyone with her remarkable dancing and arouses the jealousy and hatred of King Walid. [1. Gypsies — Fiction. 2. Dancing — Fiction.] I. Nolan, Dennis, ill. II. Title.   PZ7.T598Sav 1991   [E] — dc20   90-5902 CIP AC   I S B N 0 - 0 2 - 7 8 9 2 0 5 - 0

For Betty,
who was there
at the beginning
—A.T.

For little dancing
Genevieve

—D.N.

Long, long ago, a tribe of Gypsy coppersmiths and fortune-tellers roamed through the country ruled by the harsh King Walid. Most Gypsies were not wanted in the land. But this tribe was welcome because the chief's young daughter, Savina, inspired everyone with her dancing.

All went well with the tribe until the autumn they camped near King Walid's castle. While the chief, Kalo, and the men mended the king's kettles and made new ones, his wife, Tinka, and the women were invited into the queen's chambers. There they told the fortunes of the queen and her entourage by reading palms and tarot cards.

The children went about begging. But Savina, accompanied by Marco, a gray-bearded guitarist, danced in the kitchen. At first the servants watched, spellbound. Soon, however, aroused by her joyful spirits, they, too, were dancing.

When word about Savina reached him, King Walid sent for her. He greeted her with a scornful smile as she entered his chambers, hugging her tambourine.

"Surely you do not expect me to believe that anyone would find this motley creature captivating," he said. But the king soon saw that Savina's black slanting eyes shone with an inner glow. His heart skipped a beat, and his smile turned to a scowl.

Marco struck a chord on his guitar, bowed, and then began to strum its strings. Savina dropped a deep curtsy while slowly beating her tambourine with sharp raps. Then, thinking of squirrels at play — flicking their tails, leaping about the branches of a tree, and chasing each other around and around its trunk — she began to dance. She circled the room faster and faster, spinning and leaping on flashing feet that seemed never to touch the floor.

As he watched, the king's scowl deepened. They will flock to that urchin like moths to a flame, he said to himself. Anyone with such control over my people is a danger to my throne.

And a cold finger of fear touched his heart. He decided that he had to keep Savina where she could be watched.

"You do our girl child a great kindness, Your Highness," said Kalo when the king suggested that Savina live in his castle. "But she is a Gypsy."

"It is the way of Gypsies to sleep under the stars," said Tinka.

"A tent will be erected in my courtyard for her," said the king.

"Our girl child would not be happy sleeping in the same court-

yard night after night," said Kalo, drawing Savina to him. "For hundreds of years, we Gypsies have wandered the earth."

"I would feel like a caged bird," said Savina.

The king wanted to force Savina to stay at his court. He could see, however, that she had won the queen's heart, and the queen would make things miserable for him if he did. But as soon as he dismissed the three Gypsies, he began to plot a way to get custody of Savina without his wife's knowledge.

Those Gypsies prize their freedom above everything, he thought. If I devise a way to take it from them, they will soon compel Kalo to deliver that wretched creature into my power.

"It is not in me to trust King Walid," Kalo told his people the next morning.

"Anyone who opposes a king's wishes does not go unpunished," said Marco. "Remember how Cousin Manfo wasted away in prison after refusing to become a court musician?"

Kalo nodded. "The king may yet send his soldiers to seize Savina. Let us be off."

But just as they began to hitch up the wagons, the king's horsemen swooped down upon the Gypsies.

"Hide!" cried Tinka, shoving Savina under a wagon.

"King Walid has decreed that unless you surrender your daughter to him, Gypsies may no longer have horses," the captain told Kalo.

"Do not talk to us of giving up Savina," said Kalo. "That we will never do."

Moments later, the soldiers were leading the Gypsy horses away.

"We must move on," said Kalo when the soldiers had gone.

"How can we?" protested Savina, creeping out from under the wagon. "We have no horses."

"We will do as Gypsies did long ago," said Kalo. "We will walk."

"It's all my fault," cried Savina. "I must go back to the king."

"No! No!" said Tinka, hugging Savina.

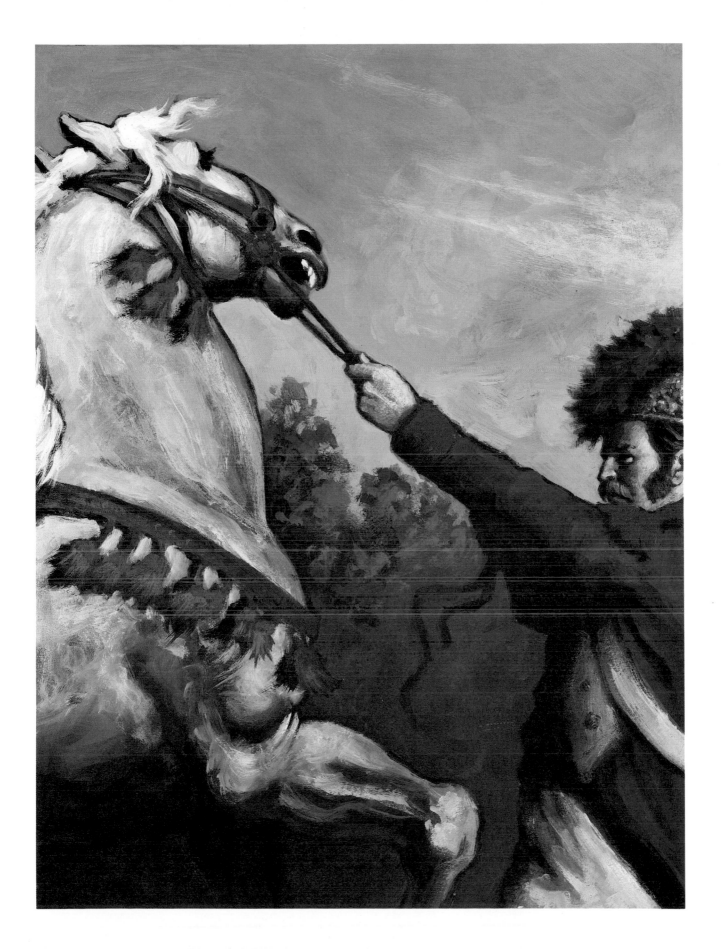

The Gypsies packed their tents and other belongings and carried them on their backs, leaving their wagons behind. Soon after they had set out, chilling autumn rains swept down from the north, soaking the travelers to the skin. But their spirits were not dampened, and they pressed on, stopping along the way to mend kettles and tell fortunes.

As night crept over them, they set up camp near a quick-running brook at the edge of a wood. Soon stews were simmering in black caldrons swung over open fires. And after all had feasted to the fullest, they clamored for Savina to dance.

"I cannot," cried Savina. "It will bring more trouble."

"The blame for losing our horses is not yours," said Marco.

"Kings have always harried us," said Bibi, his wife. "If it weren't your dancing, it would be something else."

Marco struck several rousing chords on his guitar. The Gypsies clapped their hands and stamped their feet. The air throbbed with their joy of life. And Savina, in spite of her resolve not to dance, caught their spirit. Around and around the high-flying fires she leaped and twirled, faster and faster. The Gypsies flocked about her, until they all formed a giant swirling kaleidoscope of color under the silver moon.

When King Walid realized that losing their horses had not forced the Gypsies to surrender Savina, his fear of her grew. He wasted no time in conceiving another plan.

"Let us see how long they protect her when they have no tents," he said.

And under his orders, the king's horsemen sought out Kalo's tribe. Early one evening they swooped down upon the Gypsies' camp and ripped their tents to ribbons.

"Please send me to the king," Savina begged Kalo after the soldiers had left. "It pains me to see everyone suffer."

"Do not trouble yourself," said Marco, who was mending his guitar. "With us Gypsies, a danger to one is a danger to all."

A smile wreathed Bibi's weathered face. "And just think," she said. "Our loads will be much lighter without tents."

"Who has need of a tent?" cried Kalo, grabbing a stout stick.

"We'll dig holes in the ground just like the Gypsies of long ago," cried Marco, grabbing another stick.

Soon all the Gypsies were raking the ground with stout sticks. Laughing and joking, they competed to see which family would be first to finish digging a pit.

Even though winter had blanketed the ground with deep snow and the wind cut through their clothes like knives, the Gypsies forged their way to villages and towns, where Savina could dance. She was such a bright spot on the dull winter scene and she so warmed the hearts of the people with her joy of living that they showered her with coins of copper, silver, and sometimes gold.

When King Walid heard that the Gypsies were still happy and carefree although he had left them with nothing, his fear of Savina's power filled his every waking moment. And he became convinced that she was a witch.

"The Gypsies will never surrender her to me," he said. "She must be destroyed. She and all her tribe will be destroyed."

Soon after the soldiers had started to search for the Gypsies, Kalo learned of the king's plan from one of the people whose heart Savina had captured.

"It is time to shake King Walid's sand from our feet," Kalo declared.

"The new moon has come," said Tinka as the Gypsies set out that evening. "May she be lucky for us."

To confuse their pursuers, some Gypsies walked backward; some walked forward. And each family took a different route to a gathering place in the pine forest a day's journey from the border of a neighboring country.

The king's soldiers marched first one way, then another.

"They move like the wind," complained the army commander.

Keeping out of sight, the Gypsies pressed onward, not stopping to eat or rest except at night. For a week they traveled, until all the families reached the gathering place in a clearing deep in the pine forest. It was almost dark when the last weary family arrived. As they shaped the snow into shelters, they grew cheerful and talked of leaving King Walid's country behind the next day.

"There is not a sign of the king's army anywhere," said Kalo. "Let us celebrate."

But soon after the smoke of their campfires was curling toward the sky, a gunshot rang out nearby. There followed a second shot, and a third.

"They're close upon us," cried someone.

"We're doomed!" cried another.

"Doomed. Doomed. Doomed," droned throughout the camp.

Savina ran to her father. She had to persuade him to let her do what she must.

Moments later the Gypsies faded into the forest and Savina stood alone amid the campfires. She heard gunshots from the right, from the left, from everywhere. Fear squeezed her heart as she peered at the trees.

Could she gladden the hearts of the soldiers long enough for her people to escape? Why hadn't she let Marco stay with her? His music always sparked her joy in dancing. Then she glimpsed faces in the trees that circled the clearing. The moment had come. She rapped her tambourine.

Around and around the fires she danced, swaying, leaping, whirling on flashing feet. And as she danced she caught a blurred picture of soldiers standing around the edges of the clearing with guns. Faster and faster she danced, waiting for the hail of bullets.

But the soldiers, tired from their long search, were so enchanted by Savina's dancing that they did not shoot. Slowly, first one, then another dropped his gun and drew nearer to Savina. When a soldier was close enough, she took him by the hand and set him to whirling with her. Then one by one she set the rest of the soldiers whirling. Soon all were dancing.

On and on Savina and the soldiers danced. The fires died out. Slowly the soldiers dropped, exhausted, to the ground until, just before dawn, Savina had vanquished them all. Then, with quick-footed steps, she rejoined the tribe.